Kitty on the Farm

By Phyllis McGinley

Illustrated by Feodor Rojankovsky

formerly titled *A Name for Kitty*

A Golden Book • New York
Western Publishing Company, Inc., Racine, Wisconsin 53404

Once, on a farm in the country, there
lived a little boy who was given a brand-new
kitty to be his very own. But she had no name
and the little boy didn't know what to call her.

So he went to his mother and asked,
"Mother, what shall I call my kitty?"
His mother was busy making a cake, and
she gave the little boy the spoon to lick.

"Why don't you call her Tiger?"
"Oh, no," said the little boy, "I can't call
her Tiger. She's not that big."
So he went to find his father.

"Father," he asked, "what shall I call my kitty?"

His father was busy mending a fence, and he gave the little boy a hammer to hold while he put a board in place.

"Why don't you call her Shoe-leather, because she's bound to be always underfoot?"

"Oh, no!" cried the little boy. "That name's too long."

So he turned back to the house to find his grandfather.

His grandfather was sitting on the porch,
and he wasn't busy at all.

"Grandfather," asked the little boy, "what
shall I call my kitty?"

"Wait a jiffy until I get my thinking cap,"
said his grandfather.

And he went inside to get his bright red thinking cap. "Why don't you call her Joseph, because she has a coat of many colors?"

"But Joseph is a boy's name and this is a girl kitty," said the little boy.

The little boy wandered back down the path. "If my mother doesn't know and my father doesn't know and neither does my grandfather," the little boy said to himself, "perhaps I could find out from the animals on the farm."

So he went to the stile and he climbed
right over, and he asked of the cow who was
nibbling at the clover,
   "Cow, what shall I call my kitty?"

"Moo," lowed the cow, shaking her horn at a butterfly. "Moo, moo-oooo."

"Moo!" said the little boy. "That's no name for a kitty."

So he hurried to the barnyard as fast as
he was able, and he asked of the horse, at
dinner in the stable,
"Horse, what shall I call my kitty?"

"Neigh," whinnied the horse, politely
looking up from his oats. "Neigh, neighhhhh."
"Neigh!" exclaimed the little boy. "That's
no name for a kitty."

So he walked by the garden, all alone, and
he asked of the dog who was burying a bone,
  "Dog, what shall I call my kitty?"
The dog stopped scraping for a minute.

"Bow-wow, bow-wow-wow," he barked.
"Bow-wow. Bow-wow, indeed!" cried the
little boy crossly.
"That's no name at all for a kitty."

So he crossed the pasture to the hill
below, and he asked of the sheep who were
grazing in a row,

"Sheep, what shall I call my kitty?"

"Baa," bleated the sheep, all raising their
heads in the same direction at the same
time. "Baa."

"Baa," sighed the little boy. "I might have known. That's no name for a kitty."

So he went to the chickens to try his luck,
but the chicks said "Peep" and the hens said
"Cluck."

And "Quack" said the duck when he asked the duck.

And the pig just grunted as if he hadn't heard.

And the fish in the fish pond *didn't say a word.*

So the little boy sat down sadly on the
back doorstep in the sunlight and put his
chin in his hand and he thought and he
thought and he thought.

The kitty chased a sunbeam and purred.
"Kitty," murmured the little boy. "Nice
kitty. Here, kitty, kitty, kitty."
And then all of a sudden he jumped up.

"I know!" he shouted happily. "I know what
I'll call my kitty. I'll call her Kitty."
And he did.